Grampa Sam

A Tail of Many Tales
From
the Land of Barely There

by

Stephen E. Cosgrove

Illustrated by

Wendy Edelson

DreamMaker

111 Avenida Palizada West
San Clemente, CA 92672

The Tails of Many Tales
From
The Land of Barely There

Dedicated to the delightful memory of Sam Walton, and the sage advice he gave me. I found him as wise as any of the silvered hares in the land of Barely There.

Stephen

About web-enhanced SakesAlive Books

This is one of many stories from the land of Barely There. Like all stories it contains a beginning a middle and an end. Unlike other stories you have read the story continues on the internet at a site called SakesAlive™:

http://www.sakesalive.com

When you have finished reading Grampa Sam visit SakesAlive and continue your adventure by writing letters to the characters in this book.
If you write them they will answer you in kind with a very unique and very special e-mail from SakesAlive.

My oh my, SakesAlive
characters are living
and here they thrive.
My, oh my, SakesAlive!

sakesalive.com

arther than far
and to the very edge of
the horizon was a path bordered in lacy
fern.
    If you followed that path you would
find the land of Barely There.

Barely There...

...a land where crickets sing as the sun goes down and chipmunks dance like furry little clowns.

Barely There...

...where the scented summer winds whisper gently through trees, "Barely There! Barely There!"

If you followed the path on through the Whisper Forest, past Tattertown and over Biltfast Bridge you would come to a fork in the path. If you went to the left you would end up smack in the middle of the Piddle Pine Forest. But, if you turned to the right, you would eventually come to the northern end of the Lacy Fern Path; open meadows bordered in fields of wild carrots and buttonbow roses.

Here, at the base of the Mountains of Kota Kazoo, you would find round heavy-hewn doors of cedar that led down into the burrows where the bunnies lived. The burrows were warm and cozy and protected the rabbits from the thunder storms that ravaged the meadows without fail late in the summer.

Here in the burrows, twisted tunnels laced beneath the meadow like a maze leading from one bunny's home to another.

Root and vine covered the ceiling of the tunnels, and on the walls bees wax candles flickered, wax dripping on the earthen floor. Although the cave-like tunnels were a bit damp, they served their purpose well.

But the younger bunnies didn't like the burrows at all. They thought the tunnels were dark and dank. They yearned to live in the meadows above, under the open sky.

The leader of the younger bunnies was called Derby Downs. "I feel like a worm down here," he would grumble." "We need to live in the meadows in cabins like the other folk of Barely There!"

The wisest rabbit living in the burrows was a gray hare, nearly as old as dirt, who everyone called Grampa Sam. He listened politely as Derby and the others complained about the burrows.

Finally, with the coming of summer, he could take no more and offered, "Listen, lad, when I was a boy there was another young rabbit, just like you, who was bound and determined to live above the ground in the meadow. Despite warnings from the older, wiser rabbits this rabbit rabble-rouser talked everyone into building cabins above ground."

He paused and scratched his fuzzy chin and then continued, "Well, let me tell you, the summer storms came as they always do, raging down the mountains of Kota Kazoo and blew every one of those cabins down. Eeeyup, every danged one! No, lad, the burrows are better!"

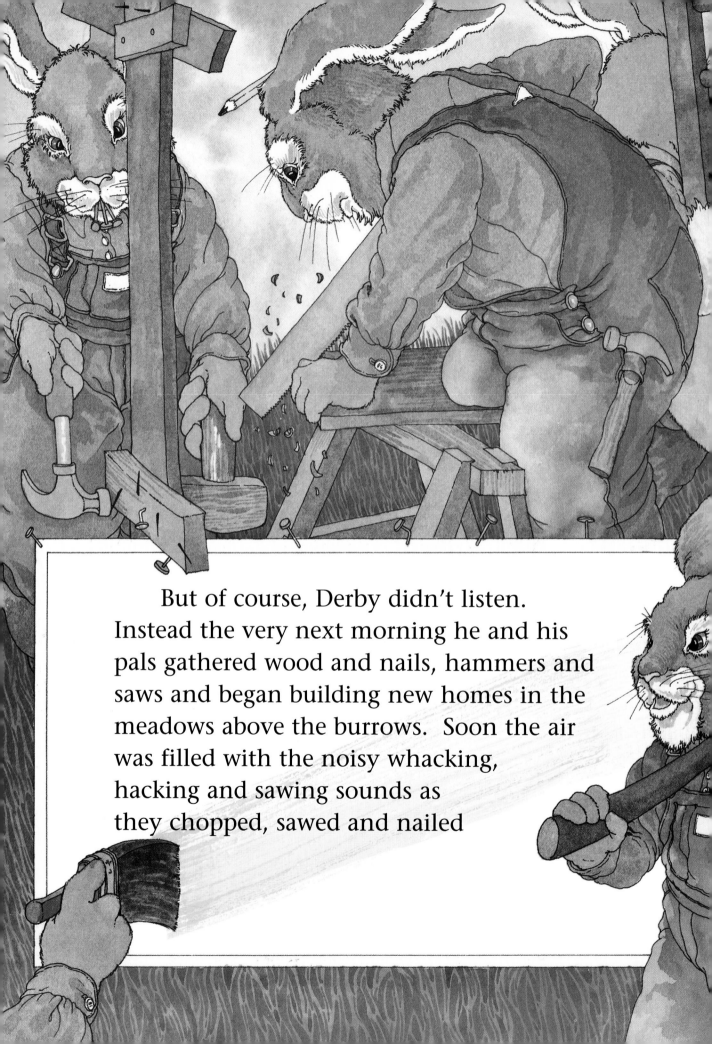

But of course, Derby didn't listen.
Instead the very next morning he and his
pals gathered wood and nails, hammers and
saws and began building new homes in the
meadows above the burrows. Soon the air
was filled with the noisy whacking,
hacking and sawing sounds as
they chopped, sawed and nailed

board to board building their dream.

Eventually the noise seeped down into the burrows and woke the older bunnies. They quickly dressed and then hippled and hoppled up the tunnels and to the meadows above. Once there they couldn't believe what they saw.

The young rabbits knew they were there, but they simply ingnored them and kept working away.

Grampa Sam shook his head as he hopped over to where Derby was working. "Listen to me," he said. "You must stop this foolishness immediately! Why, when I was a boy there was a rabble-rousing rabbit who made this same foolish mistake. Believe me, the summer storm will come raging down from the mountains!"

Derby felt as though he had listened quite enough, and with eyes snapping he said, "When you were a boy, Grampa Sam, there were still dinosaurs, and rabbits didn't live in burrows, they lived in caves. Worse than worse you still want *us* to live in caves. Well, we aren't going to live in caves anymore!"

"But, but," sputtered Grampa Sam, "when I was a boy, young rabbits listened to the old gray hares!"

"Then," laughed Derby loudly so that all could hear, "the older hares must have had something to say worth listening to! Now, if you don't mind, you are in my way. Go back to your damp burrow. I have a cabin to build!"

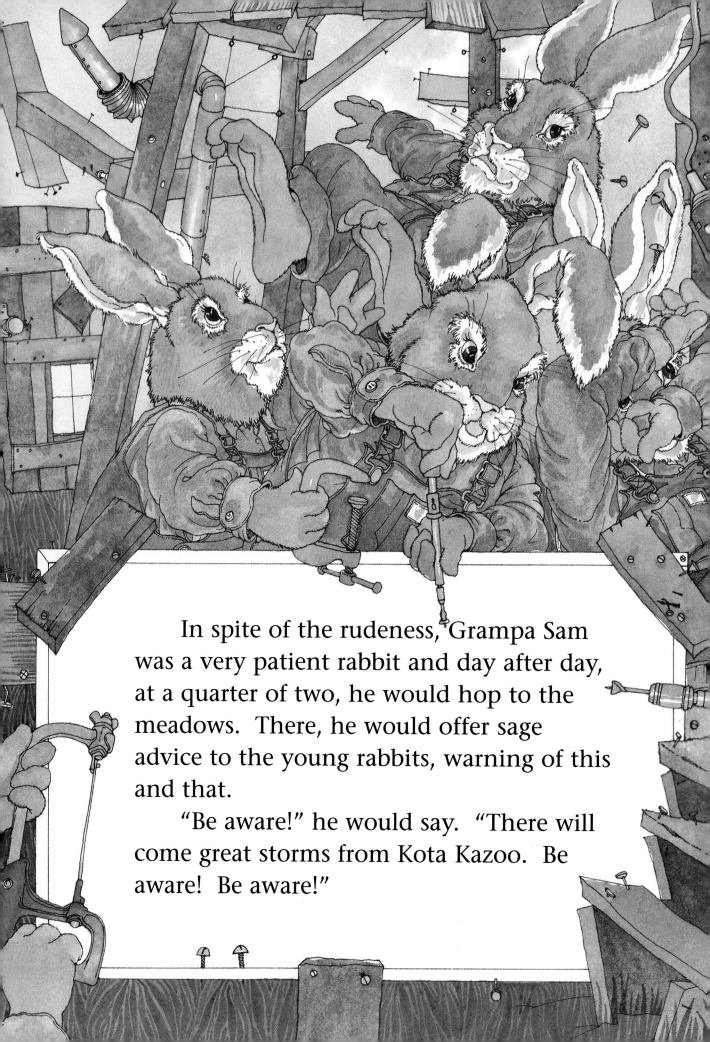

In spite of the rudeness, Grampa Sam was a very patient rabbit and day after day, at a quarter of two, he would hop to the meadows. There, he would offer sage advice to the young rabbits, warning of this and that.

"Be aware!" he would say. "There will come great storms from Kota Kazoo. Be aware! Be aware!"

But Derby and his pals wouldn't listen, rudely pretending he wasn't even there. They would chisel and chop and hammer and hack this board to that board, and for the most part, the noise drowned out anything and everything Grampa Sam had to say.

All was going just as Derby had planned!

Day after day the young bunnies continued to build the cabins in the open meadow. And day after day, the old gray hares would watch and worry about what was going to happen when the storms came. Standing in the warmth of the sun they would '*cluck*' and '*tsk*' about this and that.

"*Tsk*! *Tsk*! *Tsk*! Their houses will never stand against the wind!"

"Oh, me! Oh, My! Why can't they just live below in the burrows?"

"Why won't they listen to what we have to say?" But the noise was too loud and the younger rabbits couldn't or wouldn't listen to what their elders had to say.

Now, as it always was in the Land of Barely There in the late part of the summer, thick, angry clouds began to gather around the mountains of Kota Kazoo. With the coming of the dark rolling clouds, the wind began to blow -- a gentle warning to the meadows below.

Then, without further warning, it began blowing harder and harder!

Even below the ground the wind slipped under the massive doors -- wisps and eddies, a small taste of things to come. The older bunnies knew that a big storm was brewing, and they hoppled quickly into the meadow to give warning.

As they hopped along the winds began to howl and rumbling thunder echoed in the mountains.

"Derby, Derby!!" shouted Grampa Sam over the roar of rising wind. "The summer storm is here! You must hurry to the safety of the burrows! Hurry now, there is little time!"

"There is little to 'hurry' or worry about," laughed Derby to the other young bunnies. "A little wind can do us no harm!"

"But this is no little wind," protested Grampa Sam.   "This is the big summer storm from Kota Kazoo."

"Then you best go hide," laughed Derby as he turned back to his work.

Sadly the old gray hares hopped back to the burrows where there would be protection from the storm.

The old rabbits hadn't been gone but a moment or two when the storm blasted-down from the mountains of Kota Kazoo! Lightening flashed, thunder crashed, and the winds began to blow.

The storm, like a mighty fist, smashed into the meadow with a force and fury that was frightening to behold.

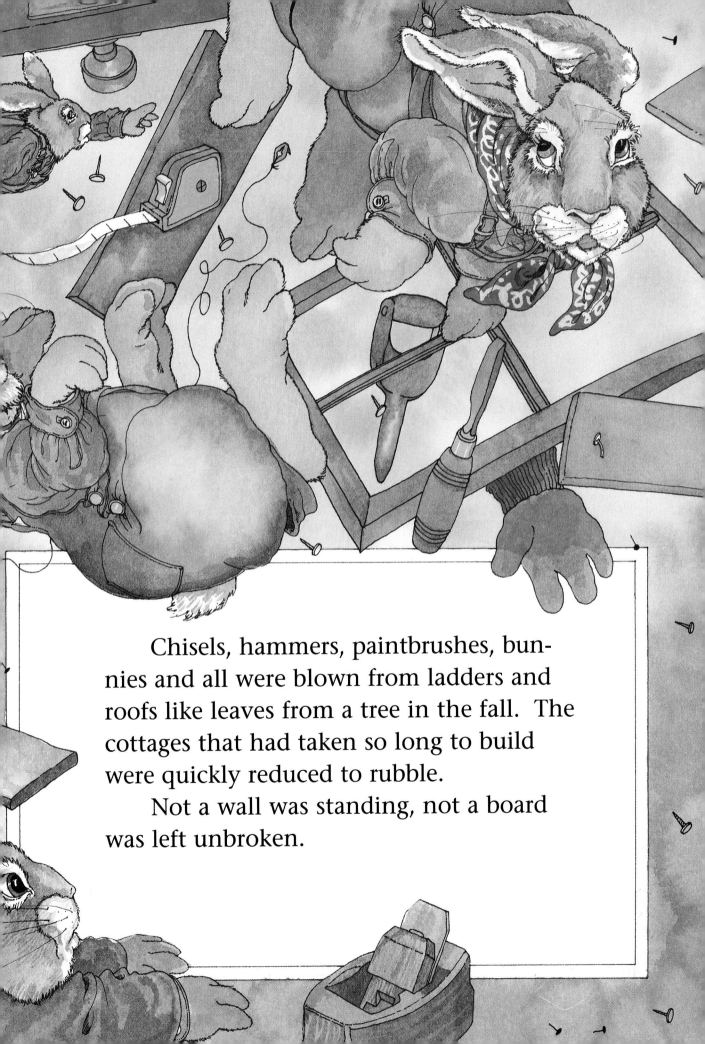

Chisels, hammers, paintbrushes, bunnies and all were blown from ladders and roofs like leaves from a tree in the fall. The cottages that had taken so long to build were quickly reduced to rubble.

Not a wall was standing, not a board was left unbroken.

Then, as quickly as it had begun, the
storm, like a wickless candle, blew itself out.
All was quiet and still.
Then the velvet-like quiet was torn with
the soft cries of hurt from the bunnies who
hung from the branches of the trees where
they had been blown!

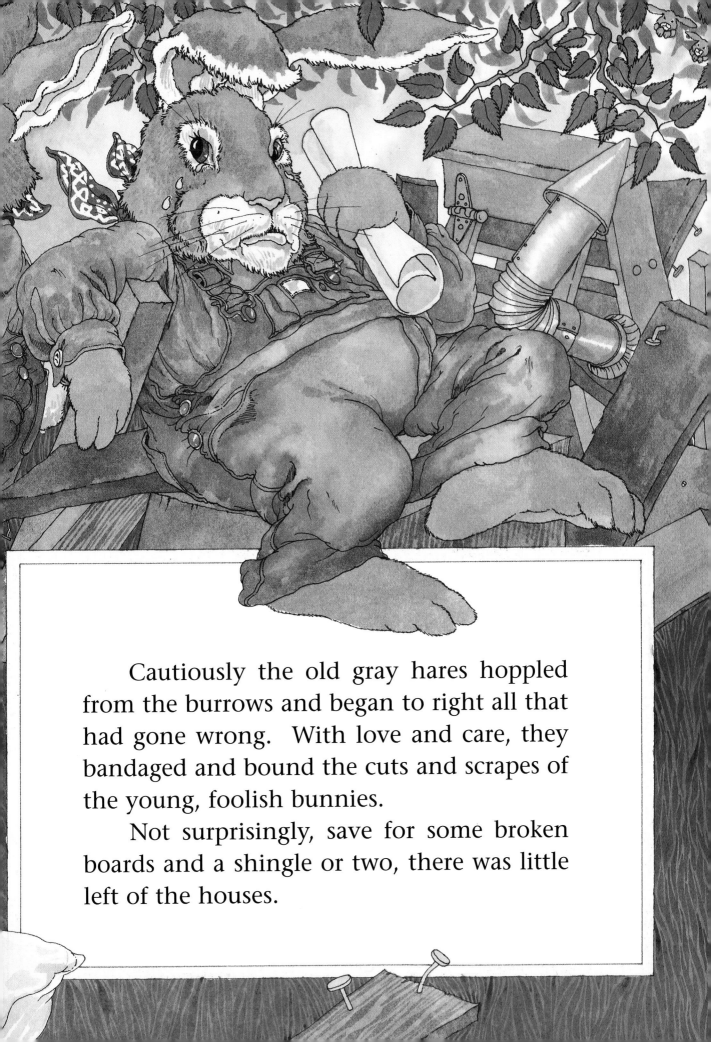

Cautiously the old gray hares hoppled from the burrows and began to right all that had gone wrong. With love and care, they bandaged and bound the cuts and scrapes of the young, foolish bunnies.

Not surprisingly, save for some broken boards and a shingle or two, there was little left of the houses.

The least hurt, but most injured was Derby Downs. He had not a scratch nor a cut, but his pride was deeply bruised. With a tear in his eye he said, "Grampa Sam I am sorry that I didn't listen. I was so very-wrong!"

"Eeeyup," consoled Grampa Sam as he patted the young rabbit on the shoulder. "When I was a boy, there was a young rabble-rousing rabbit who challenged the rules and wouldn't listen, either. He was bound and determined to live above ground. He, like you, built cabins and cottages in the meadow ignoring the warnings about the mighty storms from Kota Kazoo. He like you was foolish and didn't listen to the wisdom and experience of the old gray hares."

He smiled at Derby and then went on, "and that foolish young rabbit was me!"

From then and thereafter every evening when the sun went down, rabbits, young and old, would gather round and listen to Grampa Sam tell the wonderful stories that all began, "When I was a boy...

...in the Land of Barely There."

Now that you've read this story true,
come to web and we'll share with you.
There on a site called SakesAlive
you'll find the characters bright and alive.
Write them a letter, one maybe two,
and each in turn will write back to you.

My oh my, SakesAlive
characters are living
and here they thrive.
My, oh my, SakesAlive!

www.sakesalive.com